The Great Brain Robbery

Axel Feinstein

Look out for more stories
about Axel Feinstein!

The Great Escape

The Great Brain Robbery

Alan MacDonald
Illustrated by Lizzie Finlay

This edition produced for the Book People Ltd,
Hall Wood Avenue, Haydock, St Helens WA11 9UL

First published by Scholastic Ltd, 2002
This edition published by Scholastic Ltd, 2005

Text copyright © Alan MacDonald, 2002
Cover and inside illustrations copyright © Lizzie Finlay, 2002

ISBN 0 439 95502 5

Printed and bound by Nørhaven Paperback A/S, Denmark

CHAPTER ONE
Quiz King

Axel blamed Mr Crump. One morning in the first week of term, he'd said, "Who'd like to be in the school quiz team?"

Axel's hand had shot into the air before Mr Crump had even finished the sentence.

As usual Crump ignored him. "Darren," he said. "You seem very keen."

The class groaned. Darren Blott was as dim as a low energy light bulb.

Axel's arm stretched higher, trying to attract his teacher's attention.

Crump addressed the girl in a football shirt sitting next to Axel.

"Trudy," he said. "I'm sure you won't let us down."

"OK," said Trudy. "But what about Axel? He'd be brilliant."

The class all voiced their agreement. "Yeah, pick Axel. Axel should be in the team."

Everyone knew Axel Feinstein was the brainiest boy in the school. His head was so stuffed with ideas, his hair had to grow upwards to make room. Maybe that was why Mr Crump couldn't stand him. It wasn't just the way Axel helpfully corrected his teacher's spelling in front of the class. It wasn't the way he answered questions before Crump had even thought of them. It was Axel's habit of disrupting lessons by making the class laugh. Like the time Crump shouted, "Keep out of my sight!" and Axel had obediently walked behind him for the rest of the day.

Or the time the teacher had asked the class to bring in things from the 1940s and Axel had dragged in his granny.

Mr Crump regarded Axel as a time-bomb ticking away at the back of his class. That was why he didn't want him on the school quiz team. Not if he could prevent it.

"All right, Feinstein," he said with a cunning smile. "If you're so clever, answer me this."

He flicked through his *Bumper Book of Mind-boggling Questions* under his desk and paused at a page.

"How many toes has a rhino?" he asked triumphantly.

Axel hesitated. "The white rhino or the black rhino?"

"Either."

"Actually, they both have three, I was just interested," said Axel.

Mr Crump sighed. He knew when he was beaten.

So, by popular demand, Axel had made the school quiz team. It hardly mattered,

Crump told himself. Potter End had a noble tradition of dismal failure in every competition they entered. The Quiz Challenge wouldn't be any different.

But Crump was wrong. With Axel on the team, results over the next four weeks defied expectations. Potter End waltzed through the first round. They breezed through the second, third and fourth rounds. By half-term they had reached the dizzy heights of the semi-final. Here they came up against tougher opponents – last year's finalists, Beasley School.

It was a keenly contested struggle, but with time running out, Potter End had their noses in front by a single point. The quiz-mistress read the next question with the Beasley team knowing it might be the last. If they answered correctly they could level the scores. If not, Potter End would gain the chance to seal their victory.

"What is the capital of Brazil?"

The Beasley team squirmed in their seats. They glanced nervously at their teachers. Sweat ran down their backs like raindrops, only smellier.

"What is the capital of Brazil? What is the capital of Brazil?" they asked themselves.

"I'll have to hurry you," said the quiz-mistress.

"B," squeaked the captain suddenly.

"Pardon?"

"B is the capital of Brazil."

A few sniggers rippled through the audience.

"No, sorry. I'll offer the question to Potter End."

All heads turned in the direction of the other team. Trudy, Darren and Mae Li looked blank. They glanced at Axel hopefully. Surely he would know the answer? One more point and they would be home and dry.

Axel cleared his throat. It was purely for effect really, but he couldn't help it. One hundred pairs of eyes were turned in his direction, waiting for him to speak.

"Brasilia," he said quietly.

"Correct!"

Anything further was lost as a great cheer erupted from the audience. Potter End School were declared the winners. For the first time they were through to the Quiz Challenge final. Axel's schoolmates swarmed around him, punching him on the shoulder and banging him on the back.

Strange, he thought, how people showed their gratitude by beating you black and blue.

Trudy elbowed her way through the scrum to his side. Trudy was Axel's best friend.

She had adopted him on his first day at Potter End, when she'd found him wandering the corridors looking for his classroom. Axel helped Trudy with her homework and Trudy helped Axel to stay out of trouble. They made an unlikely pair, but they stuck together like superglue.

"How's it feel to be a hero then?" asked Trudy.

"I didn't do much," said Axel modestly.

"No, that's true," said Trudy. "We answered four of the questions without you."

"I only answered one," said Darren. "And I got that wrong."

Axel remembered. Darren had said that backgammon was a kind of bacon.

He was about to suggest they get a drink when he felt himself lifted into the air and carried towards the door by his cheering schoolmates.

"I'll see you outside!" he called back to Trudy, just before his head struck the doorframe.

CHAPTER TWO
Mad, Bad and Bald

In a dingy basement flat across town, a small bald man in a white coat was watching TV. Dr Sigmund Babble had just got out of prison and was living with his mother until he could lay his hands on someone else's money. They were watching his mother's favourite quiz show: *Who Wants to Be Stinking Rich?*

"Look at that!" said Sigmund, grinding his teeth. "Sixty-four thousand pounds for answering a few measly questions. Anyone could do it."

"You couldn't," said his mother, dunking a ginger snap in her tea.

"Mother," said Sigmund. "I am a doctor. I have a Ph.D."

"Yes, in blackmail," said his mother. "They don't ask you questions about that on quiz shows."

"Ask me a question, then. Go on, any question," challenged Sigmund.

"All right. What's the name of my postman?"

Sigmund gave up and buried his head in the local newspaper. It was full of sickening stories of summer fairs and fun-runs raising money for charity. On page four, however, a photo caught his eye.

It showed a schoolboy with wild corkscrew hair surrounded by lots of smiling chins.

The report said:

Quiz King Has The Answers

Brainy Axel Feinstein is the toast of his school pals.

Super boffin Axel correctly answered an amazing 71 questions in a row to put his team into the final of the annual Inter-School Quiz Challenge. "Most of the questions were pretty simple," said modest Axel afterwards. "Luckily maths, history and nuclear physics are my best subjects."

"What a waste," grumbled Sigmund. "If I had a brain like that I'd do something useful with it. Like going on that quiz show and winning a million pounds."

No sooner had the words left his mouth than an idea struck him. An idea so fiendishly clever that only a criminal genius could have come up with it. Sigmund Babble was going to win a million pounds and the brainy schoolboy in the paper was going to help him. Think what he could do with that kind of money! He could move out of his mother's smelly flat and into a real laboratory with his name on the door.

Dr S. Babble Ph.D. (Pentonville)

Trembling with excitement, Sigmund went to a cupboard to fetch his mother's hoover.

"Hey!" said his mother. "What are you doing with that?"

"Nothing, Mummy dear," said Sigmund. "Just taking it away for some minor improvements."

A few minutes later Mrs Babble heard the sound of hammering coming from her son's room. Sigmund was at work on another one of his inventions. "Mad as a sack of rats," she said to herself.

CHAPTER THREE
Are You Sitting Comfortably?

Mr Crump was puzzled. He hadn't been told anything about a visit from a nurse.

"Oh yes," said the nurse. "It was all in the letter. All the schools are getting a visit because of the epidemic."

"Epidemic?" repeated Crump.

The nurse lowered her voice. "Nits," she said. "I shouldn't be surprised if your class were crawling with them."

Mr Crump looked through the door at his class. He had suddenly begun to feel itchy. His scalp prickled and he began to scratch himself. Nits? Come to think of it, only this morning he'd noticed Darren Blott wriggling about in his

seat. The boy never sat still. Maybe he was infested with nits. Maybe every child in his class was crawling with them. And that meant he probably had them too.

"Combs and shampoos are useless," the nurse went on. "I've brought our new machine. The Nit Exterminator 2000. One zap from that and the nits will be dropping like, well ... like nits."

"Yes, yes. Very good," said Mr Crump. "I'll send my class along to the sick room. Now, if you'll excuse me..." He headed off quickly towards the staff toilets, where he could examine his hair in the mirror.

Later that morning Axel stood in line outside the sick room.

"Why do we have to see a nurse anyway?" grumbled Darren Blott.

"Search me," said Axel. "Crump said she's checking us for nits."

"She'll find plenty of those. Sean Suggs is a right nit," said Darren.

Before Axel could reply, Trudy came out of the medical room and closed the door behind her.

"What was it like?" asked Axel. "Did she find any?"

"No," replied Trudy. "I haven't got nits. I told her not to touch me or I'd smash her face in."

Axel could believe it.

"Next!" came a shrill voice from behind the door.

"That's you, Axel," said Trudy. "Good luck."

The nurse was certainly no oil painting. Axel's gaze took in a pair of thick hairy legs tottering on a pair of very high heels. She had curly blonde hair and red lipstick that had missed the target.

When she smiled
her mouth revealed
a glittering row
of gold fillings.

"And what's your name, young man?"
she asked in a high-pitched voice.

"Axel Feinstein," replied Axel.

"Ahh," said the nurse, eyeing him with
interest. "The quiz genius himself."

"How do you know that?" asked Axel.

"Oh … I read it in the paper," said the
nurse quickly. She cleared her throat. Axel
noticed that, up close,
her chin was rough
and bristly.

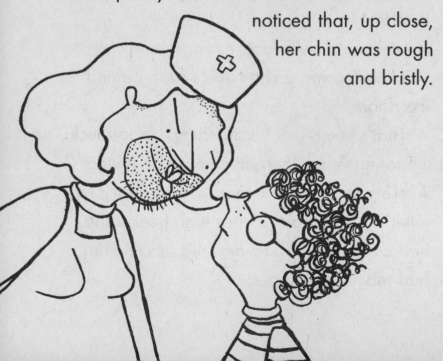

The nurse picked up a clipboard.

"Now Axel, just a few questions to start with. Who wrote *David Copperfield*?"

"Charles Dickens," answered Axel without hesitation.

"What's the longest river in India?"

"The Ganges."

"Who discovered gravity?"

"Isaac Newton," answered Axel.

"Excellent, your brain seems to be in working order," said the nurse, ticking off his answers. "Come over here and sit down."

She patted a leather chair. Above the headrest Axel could see a square-shaped helmet. It reminded him oddly of the mouth of a hoover. The helmet sprouted two aerials and had a red switch on one side. It was connected by a long curly wire to a box-shaped machine with flashing lights and rows of buttons. The machine had a small dark screen. Across this a wavy line ran, giving off occasional "blip" noises.

Axel had seen similar machines on hospital
TV series – but nothing quite as strange as this.

"What's that?" he
asked curiously.

"That? It's the Nit Exterminator 2000. It's
new, only just been invented."

"How does it work?" asked Axel, who was
fascinated by all new inventions.

"Well, the helmet goes on your head. And
if you've got nits they show up on the nit
detector here," said the nurse, pointing to the
screen. "The more nits you've got, the more
this line jumps about."

"Clever," said Axel. "But how does it get rid of the nits?"

"A small electric current runs through these wires into the headset," said the nurse. "Perfectly harmless to humans, but deadly to nits."

Axel sat down in the leather seat. He was a little surprised when the nurse started to strap him in with heavy buckles.

"Are you sure it's safe?" he asked a little nervously.

"Perfectly," said the nurse. "I've tried it on my own mother. Just sit back and make yourself comfortable."

Axel sat back.

The nurse fixed the helmet on to his head.
She fiddled with the dials next to the
screen, making adjustments.

"Anything show up on the screen?"
asked Axel.

The nurse smiled, flashing her gold fillings.
"Oh yes. Plenty. Just relax. Let your mind go
blank. Totally blank. Heh heh!"

The nurse flicked the red switch on the helmet. A loud humming sound filled Axel's ears. It grew louder and the helmet began to vibrate alarmingly. The next moment Axel felt as if the contents of his head were being sucked out by a giant vacuum cleaner. (This wasn't too far from the truth.) A searing pain shot through his skull.

The reason for the straps became clear as he tried to leap out of the chair and escape.

"Arghhh! My head!"

At last the nurse turned the machine off and the humming sound stopped.

"Now, Axel," she said. "Tell me again. What is the longest river in India?"

Axel stared back at her blankly. "Yum yum, bubble gum," he said in a dull voice.

"Excellent, you mindless moron. Toddle off back to your classroom now. Nurse has finished with you. Bye bye!"

Axel left the room, once he'd worked out how to turn the door handle.

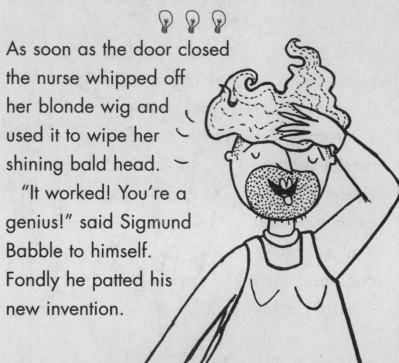

As soon as the door closed the nurse whipped off her blonde wig and used it to wipe her shining bald head.

"It worked! You're a genius!" said Sigmund Babble to himself. Fondly he patted his new invention.

The Nit Exterminator 2000, as you may have guessed, was in fact nothing to do with nits. What Babble had invented was a Brain Drainer, which had just extracted all the useful knowledge from inside Axel's head. Every single fact that Axel knew was now stored inside the helmet's micro-computer. With the help of the Brain Drainer, Babble would be able to answer any question that was put to him.

"Now for the quiz show. The money's as good as mine!" he cackled. "One million lovely pounds." He began to dance round the room, tottering on his high heels and blowing kisses to himself in the mirror.

Outside, Darren Blott heard the nurse's crazed laughter and turned pale. "Um ... anyone else want to go next?" he asked.

CHAPTER FOUR
Dumbstruck

Axel Feinstein was unusually quiet in the afternoon. He didn't once interrupt Mr Crump's science lesson to correct his mistakes. He appeared to be in a world of his own, staring vacantly into space. In the end Crump grew irritated by his silence.

"Feinstein," he said. "Are you with us?"

"Mmm?" said Axel. "Don't go away. We'll be back after the break."

"What are you talking about?"

"Exactly," said Axel. "It's just a matter of frozen peas."

There was a ripple of laughter from the class. This was more like it, Axel making Crump look a fool as usual. Axel gazed round at his classmates with a puzzled air. What was so funny? Only Trudy didn't join in with the laughter. Axel had been behaving very strangely since he'd returned from seeing the nurse. Whenever she spoke to him, he talked complete rubbish as if he were making perfect sense.

"Out here, Feinstein," Crump said, beckoning him to the front with a bony finger.

Axel got slowly to his feet. It seemed to be an effort for him to put one foot in front of the other. When he reached the front, Crump handed him a ping-pong ball. "Let's see if you've been paying attention. Explain to the class how the earth orbits the sun."

Axel stared for a few seconds at the white ball and then burst unexpectedly into song. "Chick chick chick chick, chicken, lay a little egg for me!" he sang, flapping his arms up and down and making "puck puck" noises. The class rocked with laughter. Axel had pulled off some good stunts before, but pretending to be a gibbering idiot was his best yet.

"Quiet!" shouted Crump. "Feinstein, outside, now!"

Obediently, Axel went to the window and started to climb out.

The next day the quiz team met at Trudy's house after school.

"We need to get in training," she explained to them. "The final's on Saturday, so we've only got four days to get ready."

"No sweat," said Darren Blott. "Axel's going to walk it, aren't you Axel?"

Axel nodded. "Obbly obbly onker, my fat conker," he confided.

"Very funny," said Darren. "You can stop the dumb show now, Axel. Crump isn't here."

Trudy studied Axel worriedly. She was beginning to think something was very wrong.

"Are you sure you're OK, Axel?" she asked.

"Yes sir, no sir, three bags full sir," said Axel.

"He's all right," Darren scoffed. "He's just pulling your leg. Pretending he's gone bananas to get us all worried."

Trudy wasn't so sure. She pressed the "Play" button on the video. Last night she'd recorded *Who Wants to Be Stinking Rich?* to watch as part of their training. Trudy explained that they had to try and answer the questions before the contestants on the TV.

Darren went first and got every question wrong. "What do you expect?" he grumbled. "Not a single question about football!"

Next it was Axel's turn. It was hard to get his attention at first because he'd found a Scrabble board. He was trying to build a tower with the plastic letters.

"Axel, pay attention," urged Trudy. "Listen to the questions."

On the TV screen the spotlights circled and came to rest on the next contestant. Suddenly Axel knocked over his letters and stared at the screen.

Darren Blott snorted with laughter. "Look at that idiot! What's he got on his head?"

The contestant was introduced as Dr Sigmund Babble. Sigmund was sporting a strange helmet on his head. He explained he had to wear it for medical reasons, which drew a sympathetic murmur from the studio audience. Trudy stared at him, with the odd feeling that she'd seen his face before.

"OK Siggy, first question for £100," said the quiz show host. "Blood is said to be thicker than a) Oil b) Mud c) Milkshake or d) Water?"

"Easy peas," said Trudy. "Tell him, Axel."

"Grrrr! Grrrrr!" said Axel. He crawled towards the TV on all fours, growling like a dog.

The rest of the quiz team looked at each other. This was getting beyond a joke.

If Axel was going to do animal impressions on Saturday they'd never win.

Axel barked at Babble's face on the screen. "Grr! Woof!"

Sigmund had just answered his first question correctly. His gold teeth flashed as he smiled into the camera.

Trudy jumped to her feet. "It's the nurse! The one that came to our school. I knew I'd seen those teeth before!"

"Don't be daft," said Mae Li. "That's a man."

"So was that nurse," replied Trudy. "Didn't you notice her hairy legs? It was a man in a wig. Him!"

She pointed at the screen.

Darren looked mystified. "Why would he dress up as a nurse just to check us for nits?"

"Don't be a dope," said Trudy. "The nits were just an excuse. He was after something else. The question is *what*?"

"Don't ask me," said Darren. "I only saw him for a minute."

"Me too," said Mae Li. "He hardly even looked at my hair."

"But Axel was in there ages," said Darren. "I remember because I was waiting to go next."

"Think, Darren," said Trudy, knowing she was asking a lot. "Did you hear anything while Axel was in there?"

"Yeah," said Darren slowly. "A sort of humming noise. Like a machine."

"I knew it!" said Trudy. "He did something to Axel. That funny helmet on his head. I saw it in the room. I bet that was the humming noise you heard, Darren."

"You mean, that's why Axel's been acting so funny?" asked Mae Li.

Trudy nodded. "It started when he came back from seeing the nurse. Something happened. I know it did."

They all looked at Axel who was playing with his plastic letters again. Trudy noticed that he'd arranged them into words on the carpet.

"Woof!" he said, as if he wanted to wag his tail.

"B-R-I-A-N T-O-O-K," Trudy read.

"Brian Took?" said Darren. "We don't know anyone called Brian Took."

"Maybe it's not Brian, it's brain!" suggested Mae Li.

"Yes!" said Trudy excitedly. "Brain ... took. He took Axel's brain!"

They all gaped at Axel, then at the TV.

Was it possible? Had Sigmund Babble really stolen Axel's brain? It would certainly explain why Axel had turned from a genius into a total dimwit. And why Babble was wearing a strange helmet on his head.

On the TV show, Babble had answered every question correctly. It all added up, thought Trudy. Suddenly he turned up on TV answering questions as if he were a quiz genius himself. What if he were using Axel's brain to help him win a million pounds?

As the credits played out the presenter put an arm round Babble's shoulders.

"Siggy will be back tomorrow night, when he'll be just three questions away from winning a million."

"We've got to stop him," said Trudy. "It's up to us to rescue Axel's brain. And we don't have much time."

CHAPTER FIVE
Brain Raiders

Getting to the TV studio had not been easy. They'd used up all Mae Li's birthday money in order to buy the train tickets. When they arrived at the station they'd had to walk the last mile to reach the studio. Axel was a nightmare on the journey because he kept wanting to play a game of "Snap" with the train tickets.

The recording of *Who Wants to be Stinking Rich?* took place at six o'clock. They finally arrived, out of breath, at the studios, with five minutes to spare. However they hadn't bargained on the security guard at the studio door.

"Can I see your tickets?" he asked.

"Tickets?" repeated Trudy.

"For the show. No one goes in without a ticket."

"But we've got to," pleaded Trudy. "It's a matter of life and death."

"Sorry. Tickets only. That's the rule."

Trudy looked at the others, at a loss. Now what? Babble would be appearing on the quiz show any minute and they were stuck outside.

It was Axel who unexpectedly saved the day. He pressed four tickets into the hand of the surprised security guard. "Snap!" he said with a look of triumph.

They hurried past to the studio, before the security guard discovered he'd been given a bunch of train tickets.

"Listen, here's the plan," said Trudy, outside the door. "Me and Axel will sit in the audience. You two go to the back and cover the exits. When I stand up that's the signal."

"For what?" asked Darren.

"To corner Babble! We've got to get our hands on that brain machine."

Under the studio lights, Sigmund Babble sat in the black leather chair, sweating. He was so close now. Three more questions and he would be leaving with a cheque for one million pounds. The presenter leaned forward in his seat.

"How many eyes did the giant, Cyclops,

have? a) One b) Two c) Three Or d) Ten?"

Sigmund frowned – he'd never heard of Cyclops. It sounded like a bike shop.

In a row near the back, Axel sat forward in his chair. He wanted to answer the question but his words kept getting muddled.

"One, two, buckle my foot," he muttered.

People turned round in their seats. "Shhh! Quiet!"

"Shhh! Shhh!" replied Axel loudly. Trudy squirmed in her seat. Maybe it hadn't been such a good idea to bring Axel.

In the spotlight Sigmund tuned into the thoughts that came from the Brain Drainer. *How many eyes did Cyclops have?* The answer came to him as if someone had whispered it in his ear.

"It's a," he answered.

"Final answer?"

"Final answer."

The quiz-master looked solemn. "You had a hundred and twenty-five thousand pounds, Siggy ... you now have ... A QUARTER OF A MILLION POUNDS!"

Sigmund tried to look modest but couldn't help hugging himself with glee. A quarter of a million!

Just two more questions and the big prize – one million pounds – would be his. The studio audience were clapping. Sigmund waved to them. He felt like a TV star – though in fact the helmet made him look more like an alien.

With each question Axel was getting more excited.

"For five hundred thousand pounds," said the quiz-master. "How many toes has a rhino? Is it a) Five b) Four c) One or d) Three?"

Axel jumped up and down in his seat with his hand in the air. "Ooooh, Miss! Ooooh, ooooh!" he pleaded.

"Pack it in, Axel. Everyone's looking," hissed Trudy.

Glancing behind her she saw they hadn't much time. The security guard was prowling the aisle, looking for them. He must have checked their tickets and had come to throw them out. Any moment now they'd be spotted. As Trudy sank lower in her seat, Dr Sigmund Babble reached the million-pound question.

"For one million pounds," said the presenter, "who was the fourth wife of Henry VIII? Was it a) Catherine Parr b) Jane Seymour c) Anne of Cleves or d) Anne Boleyn?"

Babble closed his eyes and breathed a sigh of contentment. This would be a doddle for a brain like Axel's. The one million pounds was in the bag. Babble could almost see the bank notes raining down on him like confetti. He would buy a sports car, a speedboat, a year's supply of hair restorer.

He opened his mouth to speak...

"CHEATER CHEATER PUMPKIN EATER!"
shouted a voice from the audience.

Sigmund peered aghast into the darkness.
Someone in the audience – a boy – was
standing up, shouting at the top of his voice.
A girl in a football shirt appeared at his
shoulder and pointed accusingly at Sigmund.

"That man's a fake! He stole
my friend's brain!"

Now Sigmund remembered where he'd
seen the boy before. It was the boy genius –
Frogstein or whatever his name was – and
he'd come for his brain.

Sigmund tried desperately to tune into Axel's brain for the answer he needed. His mind was too agitated. All he could think was: why now? Why couldn't they just have waited till after the show?

In the next few seconds things happened quickly. The security guard spotted Trudy and Axel and advanced towards them. Trudy grabbed Axel's hand and pulled him along after her. They ran down the centre aisle, making a beeline for Sigmund.

Babble saw them coming. If they got their hands on the Brain Drainer it was game over.

He decided his only chance was to run
for it. He made a dash for the exit with the
helmet still on his head.
To his horror, he found
his way barred by
two more children.
Mae Li and
Darren had cut
off his escape,
just as Trudy had
instructed them.

The studio
audience was in
uproar. They hadn't
a clue what was going on but they were
ready to believe that the contestant with the
funny helmet was a rotten fake. They stood
up, booing and jeering as if it were a
pantomime. Above the noise the show's host
tried to restore order. "Please! Quiet!
Sigmund, your final answer. Can I have your
final answer?" he shouted above the din.

Sigmund Babble didn't have time for a final answer. He turned back and tried to escape up the centre aisle. Blocking his path on the stairs he met Trudy.

"Out of my way, little girl!" snarled Babble through clenched teeth.

Trudy had been called some names before, but nobody, NOBODY called her "little girl". She lowered her head and charged Babble like an angry bull. The head-butt caught him full in the stomach. Babble stumbled backwards and sat down heavily in the black leather chair. Before he could get his breath someone grabbed the Brain Drainer off his head. It was Axel. He raised the helmet high above his head like a trophy.

"Bingo!" he said.

Two security guards had reached the stage. But it wasn't Axel they were coming for. They grasped Sigmund firmly by the arm and led him away.

"This way please, sir. The police are waiting outside. They say they'd like a word with you – something about impersonating a nurse."

"One question," moaned Babble. "One question away from a million pounds."

"The correct answer was Anne of Cleves," said one of the guards. "I'd have thought you would have known that."

CHAPTER SIX
FINAL ANSWER

The whole of Potter End School was crammed into the hall for the final of the Quiz Challenge. The amazing story of Axel's stolen brain had spread like wildfire. Now everyone wanted to see if the hero of the hour could win the final for Potter End.

The Potter End team sat facing the team from Wignall Junior who had smart red sweatshirts.

"Are you sure Axel is OK?" asked Darren, for the hundredth time.

"I told you," said Trudy. "We reversed the Brain Drainer. It worked. He's got his brain back."

They both stole a nervous glance at Axel, who smiled at them.

POTTER END

Only two days had passed since Axel had been reunited with his brain. Letting him stay on the quiz team was a gamble. Mr Crump had point blank refused to let him take part. Even now Trudy could hear a muffled thumping coming from their classroom.

"It's all right," she told Mae Li. "Crump's still locked in the store cupboard."

Mae Li nodded. "Shhh! I think we're about to start."

The quiz-mistress directed the first question to Potter End. "Is a tomato a fruit or a vegetable?"

Axel's hand shot straight up in the air.

His team-mates waited, a touch nervously. Would he reply by barking like a dog?

"Yes?" asked the quiz-mistress, looking at Axel.

Axel blinked. "Oh. I'm not sure."

There was an audible groan from one hundred Potter End supporters.

"Yes I am, it's a fruit," said Axel. He grinned at his team-mates to show he'd just been pulling their legs.

Trudy kicked him under the table. "Do that again and you're dead," she muttered under her breath.

From then on the quiz final went smoothly, with Axel on top form. Mae Li and Trudy chipped in by winning the occasional point. Darren Blott contributed his usual round zero.

Wignall hadn't come this far to be beaten, however. Their team was carefully hand-picked. They'd been swotting for the final all week in the school library.

When it came to the final round of questions, Potter End found themselves trailing by two points. The score was 54-52 to Wignall.

Axel knitted his brows with concentration. He answered the next question – about cloud formations – correctly. Under pressure, the Wignall team got their next question wrong. Axel was able to answer it to claim a bonus point and level the score.

The quiz-mistress glanced at the clock. She announced that the final would be settled by a tie-breaker question. The first team to give a correct answer would win. Both teams could confer but they'd only get one chance to answer. The audience held their breath. Both teams leaned forward, alert and straining to be first with their hand in the air.

"The Toffees, the Bees and the Hatters are all what?"

Before the words were out a hand shot into the air. The hand belonged to Axel Feinstein.

"Yes? Potter End?"

Every face in the hall turned to look at
Axel. He opened and closed his mouth like
a goldfish. Nothing came out.

"Go on," hissed Trudy.

"I don't know it," whispered Axel.

"Stop messing around. Of course you do!"

"I don't! Really! I just stuck my hand up to
be first."

The quiz-mistress looked impatient. "I'll
have to hurry you."

Unexpectedly Darren Blott leaned over and
whispered in Axel's
ear. "I know it."

"What?"

"The answer.
They're all football
teams. Go on."

POTTER END

Axel took a deep breath. He knew he was about to lose his school the trophy. Listening to Darren was the dumbest thing he could do. But he didn't have any better ideas.

"Are they ... all football teams?" he asked doubtfully.

"Correct!" said the quiz-mistress. "The winner of this year's Quiz Challenge is Potter End."

The Potter End supporters gave a mighty cheer.

They came swarming forward to bang Axel on the back and punch him on the shoulder.

"It wasn't me," he tried to tell everyone. "It was Darren who got the last question."

Nobody listened of course. Darren Blott was hopeless, everybody knew that.

"Well, you're the hero, you'd better go and collect the trophy," Trudy said to Axel.

"No. Let's all go together," said Axel.

They all trooped up to the table where they were presented with the silver trophy decked in Potter End's colours. Axel, Trudy, Mae Li and Darren lifted the cup high above their heads to deafening cheers.

"Well, we did it," said Trudy. "But in future you'd better look after that brain of yours."

"I will," promised Axel. "Next time I see a nurse, I'm going to check her legs to see if they're hairy."

Trudy grinned at the thought. It sounded like trouble. But then trouble was a subject Axel knew all about.